Usborne

Stories of

Knights
& Castles

Once upon a time, brave knights rode through the land, slaying fearsome dragons and rescuing damsels in distress. The most famous of all these knights served at the court of the legendary King Arthur. They went on many quests, facing untold dangers as they battled against evil. Enter this magical world and discover the adventures of knights for yourself.

With thanks to Dr. Abigail Wheatley for her advice.

First published in 2006 by Usborne Publishing Ltd,
Usborne House, 83-85 Saffron Hill, London EC1N 8RT, England.
www.usborne.com Copyright © 2006 Usborne Publishing Ltd.
The name Usborne and the devices ♀ ⊕ are Trade Marks of Usborne Publishing Ltd.
First published in America in 2007. AE. Printed in Dubai.

Usborne

Stories of
Knights
& Castles

Anna Milbourne
Illustrated by Alan Marks

Designed by Amanda Gulliver
and Nelupa Hussain
Edited by Gillian Doherty

Contents

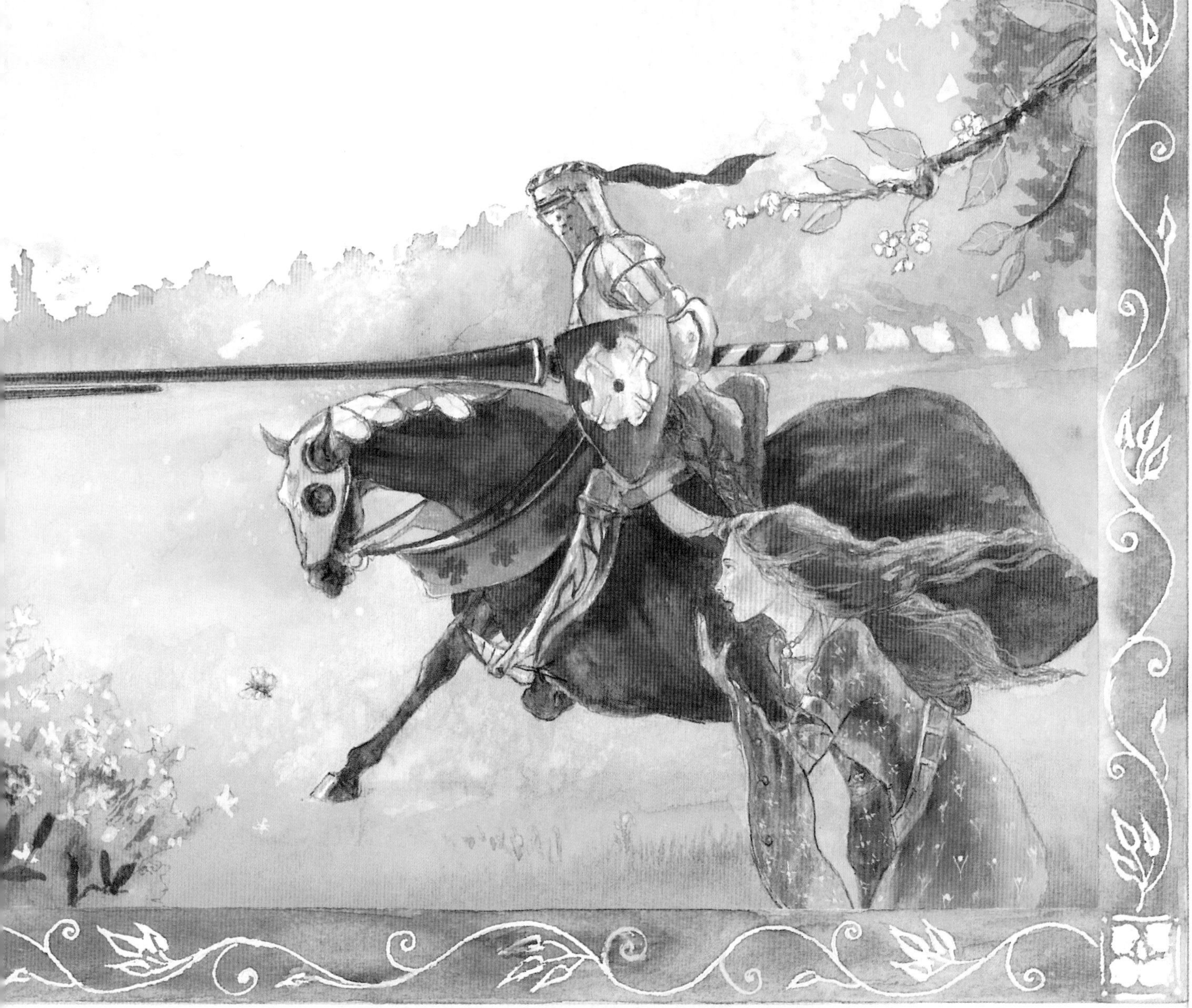

The knight
and the
lion

Once, in a long-forgotten land, a young knight set out in search of adventure. He was riding through a thick forest when, all at once, a lion hurtled past him. The very next moment, a dragon swooped down through the trees and landed, pinning the lion to the spot. Flames poured from the dragon's mouth and scorched the trapped lion's back.

Owen, for that was the young knight's name, saw that the poor creature would be burned to death unless he did something to help it, so he drew his sword and charged.

Hearing the galloping of hooves, the dragon swung its head around and blasted a jet of fire at the knight. Owen tugged on his reins and his horse swerved out of the way just in time.

As the dragon swelled its chest again, Owen darted forward and thrust his sword at its neck. The beast let out a furious bellow as the blade cut into its skin, and another blast of flames surged at Owen, forcing him to retreat.

Owen turned his horse around and charged again. This time, the dragon lashed out and knocked him to the ground. Keeping one claw on the lion, the beast lunged at Owen. The young knight steeled himself and, when the dragon was a mere shiver away, plunged his sword directly into its heart. With an ear-splitting screech, the dragon fell to the ground, dead.

Owen got to his feet and wiped its vile green blood from his sword. Then he turned to the lion. It was trembling but, strangely, it hadn't moved an inch. As he moved a little closer, Owen saw that its tail was trapped in the dead dragon's claw.

He thought for a moment or two. Then he shrugged sympathetically. "I'm sorry, but there's no other way to free you..." he said, and quickly sliced off the tip of the lion's tail.

The lion sprang away, roaring with pain. It stared at Owen wildly, and he braced himself, thinking it was about to attack. But, instead, the lion lowered its head and bowed down before him. When it looked up again, its face was bathed in tears.

"Are you *thanking* me?" asked Owen incredulously.

The lion answered by lying down and resting its head gently on the knight's feet.

"Well I never," said Owen. "I'm glad to be of assistance." Shaking his head, he got on his horse and started off through the forest. He'd only gone a little way when he realized the lion was behind him. He stopped his horse, and the lion stopped too. "Why are you following me?" Owen asked.

The lion just gazed at him with its soft, amber eyes.

Owen turned his back and trotted on through the trees. The lion loped after him. Owen sped up to a canter, and then to a gallop, but the lion kept up easily, however fast he went. In exasperation, he tried dodging through the trees to lose it, but whenever he glanced over his shoulder it was still there, padding along at his heels.

Finally, Owen stopped to rest. "It's no use following me," he told the lion sternly. "I don't know what you want." He settled down under a tree to go to sleep, and it curled up at his feet like a faithful dog.

Over the next few days, Owen got used to the big, silent creature's company. By the time he rode out of the forest, it felt like the most natural thing in the world to have a lion at his side.

The first place they came to was a walled town. Owen knocked at the gate and a thin, glum-looking gatekeeper peered out of a hatch. When he saw the lion, his eyes grew wide. "You can't bring that in here," he said nervously.

9

"Don't worry," said Owen, patting the lion's back. "He won't harm anybody."

The gatekeeper hesitated; then he shrugged his shoulders. "I don't suppose it much matters any more," he muttered, and he swung the gates open.

Inside, the town was in a sorry state. The streets were deserted, apart from a few skinny children who ran away as soon as they saw the lion. Broken market stalls lay on the ground and the houses looked badly in need of repair.

At the heart of the town stood a castle. As Owen rode up to it, the lord came outside to greet him. He was as thin and gaunt as the gatekeeper, but gave Owen a welcoming smile. "Good afternoon," he said. "Won't you come inside?"

He led Owen into a large hall where his wife and daughter were sitting sewing. When the lion appeared at the doorway, they sprang to their feet in alarm. "Don't be afraid," Owen said quickly. "He's as gentle as a lamb." As he spoke, the lion padded across the hall and lay down meekly by the fire.

"You and your lion are welcome to stay the night," said the lord, "but I'm afraid you must leave before noon tomorrow."

"What a curious thing to say," thought Owen. Then he noticed that the lord's face was pinched with anxiety, and his wife and daughter had tear stains on their cheeks. "Please tell me what troubles you," he said. "I might be able to help."

The lord sighed. "I don't think anyone can," he said bleakly. "A giant has been terrorizing our town. He's ripped up our crops and flattened our market stalls, stolen all our food and frightened our children half to death. And now…" The lord paused and his eyes filled with despair. "Now he's taken my four sons prisoner," he continued. "He's coming back tomorrow, and he's going to kill them unless I hand over my only daughter."

"Leave it to me," said Owen firmly. "I'm going to get rid of that giant for you once and for all."

The next morning, Owen rode out to meet the giant, with the lion trotting at his heels. Word about the brave stranger had spread, and the townsfolk gathered to watch him ride by. "He's so brave that even a lion looks up to him," a girl whispered to her mother as he passed them.

"Yes," replied her mother grimly, "but brave or not, he's riding to his death."

As soon as Owen and the lion went out of the town gates, the gatekeeper rammed the bolts home behind them, and all the townsfolk rushed up to the battlements to see what would happen next.

Before long, the ground began to tremble with the giant's footsteps. Dust filled the air as he thundered closer and closer. The giant was a truly terrifying sight — he was as tall as the battlements and as broad as a tower. In one enormous fist he held a club the size of a tree trunk; from the other dangled the lord's four sons. He stomped up to the town gates and peered down at Owen. "What do you want, little knight?" he boomed.

"I demand you let the lord's sons go and leave this town in peace," was Owen's bold reply. "If you don't, I'll have no choice but to kill you."

The giant threw back his head and roared with laughter. "You? Kill *me*?" he guffawed, tossing the boys down like rag dolls. "I'd like to see you try."

"Very well," said Owen, and he lowered his lance and charged. The giant roared as the lance stabbed him in the leg. He pulled it out and snapped it in two as if it were nothing but a twig. Then, purple with rage, he swung his club and knocked Owen flying.

The knight sailed through the air and landed in the dust with a thud. He lay there, dazed by the impact, and the giant stormed over to finish him off.

Just as the giant's shadow fell over the helpless knight, a blur of tawny fur shot towards him. With one incredible leap, the lion landed on the giant's back. It dug its claws into his shoulders and sank its teeth into the back of his neck.

Howling in pain, the giant dropped his club and tried desperately to shake the creature off, but the lion clung on for all it was worth, snarling ferociously.

Owen struggled to his feet. Then he drew his sword and hurled it as hard as he could. The blade whistled through the air and plunged into the giant's belly.

The giant swayed slowly to and fro, clutching his belly with both hands. Then, with a mighty groan, he toppled forwards. Owen dived out of the way just in time, and the colossal figure crashed to the ground. The earth shuddered for miles around as though an entire mountain had collapsed.

There was a long, stunned silence while the dust settled, and then a resounding cheer rose from the battlements. The gatekeeper swung open the gates, looking more pleased than Owen would have thought possible, and a jubilant crowd rushed out of them.

The lion padded over and sat down next to Owen. "Thank you for saving my life," Owen said affectionately, throwing an arm around its neck. "Whatever would I do without you?"

William's first quest

"Have you ever heard of a magic spring hidden deep in the Tangled Forest?" William asked the other knights as they sat around the fire one evening.

"Yes," answered one. "I've heard that the water boils, even though it's as cool as marble."

"And next to the spring there's a tree that never sheds its leaves, no matter what the season," another knight added. "There's a gemstone at the foot of the tree. If you sprinkle the spring water onto it, something amazing is supposed to happen."

"Well, I'm going to find that spring," William announced proudly. "It will be my very first quest."

Kay, the eldest knight, snorted. "You'll never find it," he said scornfully, "and even if you do, I bet it's guarded by some mighty knight who'll send you home whimpering."

"I'd like to see this magic spring myself," remarked King Arthur, who had come to warm himself by the fire. "Why don't we all go and find it?"

A murmur of agreement rippled around the group.

"If there is any fighting to be done," said Kay, "you'd better leave it to me."

Later, when everybody else had gone to bed, William crept out of the castle. "It was my idea to look for the spring," he muttered as he saddled his horse, "and I'm going to be the one to find it. I'll show them — I'm perfectly capable of doing my own fighting." And he galloped off into the night.

He reached the edge of the Tangled Forest just as the pale light of dawn began to appear on the horizon. "It's certainly true to its name," William thought, peering into the gloom. All he could see ahead of him were impossibly tangled branches.

He drew his sword and began to slash his way through. It was slow progress — the more he slashed, the more entangled he seemed to become. It was almost as if the trees themselves were trying to stop him from ever finding the spring. He struggled on, inch by inch, until eventually he stumbled out into a forest glade.

By this time, the sun was shining brightly in a clear blue sky. All was quiet, apart from the gentle splashing of water. There beneath a majestic pine tree was a sparkling spring. William got off his horse and cautiously dipped his hand into the water. It was as cool as marble, although the water bubbled as if it were boiling. "I've found it," he murmured, feeling rather proud of himself.

There was a small cup hanging from the pine tree, and nestled in the tree's roots was a large green emerald.

16

William filled the cup with spring water and drank thirstily. It was deliciously sweet and fresh. "Now for the moment of truth," he said, and carefully he sprinkled the last few drops of water onto the shining emerald.

There was a deafening clap of thunder and the sky turned black; then a fierce wind whipped out of nowhere and almost swept William off his feet. It whirled around, tearing up tufts of grass and howling through the trees. William clung to the pine tree for dear life. The wind pummeled and shook it, but the tree stood firm. There was a sudden flash, and a bolt of lightning struck a tree on the far side of the glade, splitting its trunk in two.

Another bolt flashed down,
and another and another,
until all the trees in sight,
except for the pine, were
splintered and destroyed.

Snowflakes began to swirl
through the air; then, seconds later,
rain and hailstones pelted down. It was as
though the sky had been torn open, and was
throwing down all of its contents at once.

Then, just as suddenly as it had begun, the storm
stopped. Everything fell quiet, the sky cleared, and the
sun shone as brightly as ever.

William was just catching his breath when there
was a rumble of galloping hooves, and a knight
burst into the glade.

William scrambled onto his horse. While he was fumbling with his reins, the knight lowered his lance and charged full-tilt in his direction. The lance struck William's shield, and William almost fell off his horse.

The knight turned and charged again, and this time William was ready. He spurred his horse into a gallop. As they thundered together, he rammed his lance so hard into his opponent's shield that the lance shattered. The knight was knocked from his saddle, but got to his feet unharmed and drew his sword.

William jumped to the ground and drew his own sword ready to fend off his opponent's attack.

As they fought, the knight drove William away from the spring. Soon, William found himself at the very edge of the glade, defending himself with desperate swipes of his sword.

"I can't fail my very first quest," he thought. He gritted his teeth and swung his sword with all his might. It struck the knight's helmet with a dull clang, making him stagger. Then, to William's surprise, he sprang onto his horse and fled.

"Wait!" called William. "I want to know who the spring belongs to." But the knight didn't stop. He hurtled along, leaping over trees that had been felled by the lightning, and William chased after him. They galloped all through the forest and out the other side.

On the edge of the forest stood a golden castle. The knight rode across the drawbridge and disappeared.

William slowed to a trot, wondering if he dared follow. Suddenly, he heard a lady's anxious voice shout, "Quickly! Fetch bandages." He heard more voices calling to one another and people hurrying around in the castle. Then everything went quiet.

A pitiful cry broke the silence. "He's dead! My best knight is dead." And somewhere in the castle, the lady began to weep. "Who will guard my magic spring now?" she sobbed.

William was horrified. "What have I done?" he thought. "I was so caught up with finding the spring that I didn't even think what would happen. Now I've killed a knight, and a lady is crying as though her heart will break."

Just then, he heard footsteps approaching. In a panic, he crouched behind a fallen tree to hide. A group of servants appeared a moment later, carrying the dead knight.

21

Behind them walked a beautiful lady, her face wet with tears. When William saw her, his heart almost leaped out of his chest with pity. "What can I do to put this right?" he said to himself.

By this time, the procession was crossing the drawbridge. Any moment now they might notice him; if he wanted to slip away, there was no time to lose. But William couldn't bring himself to leave. Instead, he took a deep breath and stepped out onto the drawbridge. "Please forgive me," he said humbly and knelt before the lady.

The lady stopped. "Who are you?" she asked in surprise.

"I'm the knight who killed the guardian of the spring," said William sadly. "But had I known what sorrow it would cause, I never would have fought him."

"I ought to have you killed right here on the spot!" the lady exclaimed.

"I am at your mercy," replied William.

"You have left me and the spring with no defense," the lady continued angrily. "Now whoever finds the spring may cause terrible storms for their own amusement. They don't care that the storms do so much damage – harming animals and ruining crops..."

"I'd like to try to make amends," said William. "If you'll let me, I could defend your spring from now on."

The lady hesitated, glancing at William's young face. "You're brave enough to admit what you did and accept the consequences of your actions," she said in a softer tone. "Perhaps you'd make a good guardian of the spring..."

Just then, there was an ominous rumble of thunder, and lightning streaked down from the sky. A furious wind whipped up, stripping the leaves off the trees and hurling branches into the air. "Now is your chance to prove yourself," said the lady urgently. "Someone has started another storm."

William leaped onto his horse at once and galloped away. When he arrived at the spring, he found King Arthur and a group of knights gathered around it. They were so absorbed that they didn't notice him ride into the glade.

Kay was standing nearest to the spring, with the cup in his hand. "If only William had seen that storm," he said smugly. "I bet he'd have run away! Shall we do it again?"

"No!" cried William, and he lowered his visor and charged.

"Watch out!" King Arthur called.

Kay hurriedly jumped onto his horse and spurred it into a gallop. But, before he knew what was happening, William had knocked him head over heels.

Kay picked himself up off the ground. "Whoever this knight is, he's strong," he said. "Are you as good with a sword as you are with a lance?" he asked William.

Without a word,
William leaped to the
ground. The two knights
fought to and fro until
Kay began to tire. He lost
his footing and, seizing the
opportunity, William
lunged at him. He knocked
the sword from Kay's hand
and pinned him against the
pine tree.

"Mercy!" rasped Kay.
William released him
at once. Then, with a grin,
he pulled off his helmet.

"Hello Kay," he said.
The older knight's eyes
almost popped out of his
head. "It's you!" he exclaimed.
Then he flushed with shame. "It seems
I was wrong, William," he admitted sheepishly.
"You've turned out to be a fine knight after all."

King Arthur stepped forward. "I never thought
any less," he said, laying his hand on William's shoulder.
"But you've proved it beyond any doubt, young William.
I'm proud to call you one of my knights."

24

The garden
of
eternal summer

One frosty winter's evening, an adventurous knight named Erec and his wife Enide were out riding when they came across a walled town perched on top of a hill.

"That's Brandigan," said Erec. "I've heard that the castle there has a magic garden of some kind."

"It sounds intriguing," Enide said. "Let's go and look." They rode up the hill and in through the town gates. Brandigan was a pretty little place; the huddled roofs were dusted with snow and warm light glowed in every window.

Erec and Enide rode through the winding streets until they reached the castle in the middle of the town. As they rode up to it, the king himself came out to greet them. "Welcome," he said. "I haven't had any visitors in such a long time. Won't you stay the night?"

"That's very kind. We'd love to," Erec replied, and Enide nodded in agreement.

"What brings you here?" the king asked as he led them inside.

"We've heard about your magic garden," said Enide eagerly. "Please may we see it?"

25

"Yes, of course you may," replied the king. His answer was friendly enough, but a mournful look had crept into his eyes.

"You look sad," said Enide. "Is something wrong?"

The king sighed. He showed them into a grand hall and asked them to sit down. "Twelve long years ago," he began, "my nephew and his sweetheart went into the garden, and I haven't seen them since. I miss them terribly. Ever since that summer's day, nothing in the garden has changed. It's as though time has been suspended."

"Hasn't anyone tried to find them?" asked Erec.

"Yes," replied the king, "but it isn't as easy as that. We'll go there tomorrow and you can see for yourselves."

In the morning, right after breakfast, the king took Erec and Enide to see the magic garden. There had been a heavy snowfall in the night and the air was bright and cold. Their horses plodded slowly through the deep snow until they came to an archway of sweet-smelling roses. "Here it is," said the king.

As Erec and Enide followed him through the archway, their eyes grew round in amazement. Inside the garden, it was as though winter had never existed. The light was warm and golden, and wherever they looked the most beautiful flowers bloomed; ripe fruit hung from almost every branch, and birdsong filled the balmy air.

26

The king plucked a peach from a tree and handed it to Enide. "Taste this," he said.

Enide took a bite out of the golden fruit and closed her eyes. "It's delicious," she murmured blissfully.

"You can enjoy everything the garden has to offer while you're here," said the king, "but anything you take outside – even the smallest flower – withers and crumbles to dust immediately. The garden seems to be protected by magic. No matter how many seasons go by, it's eternally summer here."

Erec and Enide looked around for a moment or two, lost in wonder. Then Erec cleared his throat. "What about your nephew?" he asked in a gentle voice.

The king's expression clouded with sorrow. "Come on," he said. "I'll show you." He led them between the flowerbeds, past a brimming fountain, and stopped at a grove of trees.

Enide gave a horrified gasp. Ahead of them were twelve spikes. The first eleven each had a man's skull stuck on the top. The twelfth was empty, apart from a golden horn dangling on a ribbon.

"These," said the king grimly, "are the heads of the knights who have ventured past those trees to find my nephew."

"And the last spike?" Erec asked.

"It must be for the head of the next knight who tries and fails," replied the king.

"Not if I can help it," Erec declared. "I'm going to try to find your nephew."

"Are you sure?" asked the king, but he only had to look at Erec's face to know the answer. "Then I wish you every success," he said gratefully. "We will wait for you at the castle."

Erec turned to Enide, whose face was ashen with fear, and took both of her hands in his. "Don't worry," he said. "I won't fail. I'll be back once I've completed the quest."

Enide smiled bravely. "I know," she said. "Good luck."

Erec rode between the spikes and passed through the grove of trees. Dappled sunlight shone through the leaves, and butterflies danced in the air. Beyond the trees, he found a meadow. Sitting on the grass was a beautiful girl with long, red hair and eyes as blue as the summer sky.

"Hello," said Erec.

The girl looked up at him and frowned.

Before Erec had a chance to ask what the matter was, a knight dressed in scarlet came galloping along. "You're a fool to disturb us," cried the Scarlet Knight. "Now you'll have to die like all the others." And he lowered his lance and charged.

Erec urged his own horse into a gallop. The two knights hurtled towards one another. Erec's lance hit the edge of his opponent's shield and glanced off harmlessly.

They turned their horses and charged again. This time, the Scarlet Knight's lance slammed into Erec's shield. The lance splintered with the impact, but Erec stayed firmly in his saddle.

The Scarlet Knight flung down the remains of his lance. "If you won't be beaten on horseback," he said, sounding surprised, "I'll fight you on foot." He got down from his horse and drew his sword, so Erec sprang to the ground and drew his too.

The Scarlet Knight was a brilliant swordsman, but Erec matched him blow for blow. The two knights fought determinedly for hours, until they were so exhausted they could barely stay on their feet.

The Scarlet Knight was the first to fall. Erec dealt him a powerful blow, and he stumbled to his knees. He leaned on his sword, unable to get up. "I'm too tired to fight any more," he panted.

"Don't hurt him!" cried the girl, rushing to his side.

"I don't want to hurt anyone," Erec said. "I just want to know what this is all about. Admit defeat and we can stop."

"You've won, I admit it," said the Scarlet Knight. "A fine fighter you are too. Nobody has ever beaten me before."

Erec threw himself down on the grass and pulled off his helmet. "Thank you," he said. "Now, please will you tell me your story?"

The knight nodded. "Twelve years ago, my sweetheart and I came to live in this garden," he began. "Before that, we lived in my uncle's castle. We had lots of friends and a life full of adventure. We were as happy and in love as we could ever imagine. Then, one day, my sweetheart asked me to make her a promise." He gazed at the girl tenderly. "I'd do anything in the world for her," he continued, "so I said yes."

"What did you ask?" Erec said to the girl.

"I asked him to come and live with me here. I cast a spell on the garden so that nothing inside it would ever change. That way, our love could never spoil or die. But we could never leave," the girl explained. "Only when another knight defeated my beloved in battle would it be possible to lift the spell."

Erec looked around at the garden. "It's a beautiful place to live," he said.

"It is," agreed the Scarlet Knight, "but just imagine if you could never see your family or friends again; never go on an adventure or explore new places; never watch the sun set in the evening or see the leaves turn golden at the end of summer. Love is a thing to treasure, but you can't keep it locked away."

He put his arms around the girl. "The real world has come to take us back," he said quietly.

The girl buried her face in her hands and wept as though her heart would break. "But everything will change now and our love will be lost," she sobbed.

The Scarlet Knight lifted her chin gently and looked into her eyes. "No matter what changes, my love for you will never die," he said. "Haven't you realized that yet?"

The girl gazed at him for a moment and then she smiled. She turned to Erec. "Go and sound the horn," she said. "It will lift the spell that keeps us here."

Erec walked back through the trees, and picked up the golden horn. He raised it to his lips and blew. A pure, clear note rang out, and right away the warm light began to fade. Snowflakes from the world outside floated into the garden and settled on the grass and summer flowers.

As the magic slipped away, the garden itself began to change, as though it was racing to catch up with winter. Right before Erec's eyes, fruit dropped from the trees; leaves turned fiery red and orange, and drifted to the ground; birds flew away into the sky, and water trickling from the fountain froze into shining icicles.

The knight and his sweetheart ran through the trees, snowflakes sparkling in their hair. They stopped in front of the row of spikes, and the girl touched them one by one. To Erec's astonishment, the spikes crumbled to the ground and vanished. In their place appeared eleven knights, all unhurt, rubbing their eyes sleepily.

Just then, a joyful cry rang out. It was Enide. She rushed across the garden and into her husband's open arms. "I heard the horn," she said excitedly. "You did it, Erec! I'm so proud of you."

Erec hugged her tightly. Then he looked at the red-haired girl. "Love doesn't die if you let it run free," he said softly. "If anything, it grows stronger."

"Yes," replied the girl. "I can see that now."

By this time, every last trace of the enchanted summer had disappeared and the cold of winter had set in. But as they left the garden, the red-haired girl was struck by how magical everything looked, all covered in a soft, white blanket of snow.

The best knight
and the
brave princess

All through the kingdom and far beyond, there was no better knight than Lancelot. King Arthur's knights were famous for being noble and brave, but Lancelot shone out among them. If there was ever a damsel to be rescued or a tyrant to be defeated, Lancelot was everyone's first choice.

One spring, the King of Bade invited Lancelot and lots of other knights to a jousting tournament. Striped pavilions were set up in the meadow by his castle, a delicious feast was prepared, and crowds of people gathered to watch the fun.

Lancelot was in fine fettle and won every single match he entered. "You could learn a thing or two from that fine knight," the king commented to his son, Maurice. "He's truly amazing."

Prince Maurice didn't reply, but eyed Lancelot for the rest of the afternoon, seething with jealousy.

By the time the tournament was over, Lancelot had beaten thirty-six knights in a row. The king's daughter, Elena, awarded him first prize. "Well done, Lancelot," she said. "You were a pleasure to watch."

Maurice sidled up to them. "Everybody thinks you're such a fine knight, Lancelot," he said slyly. "I suppose you *are* rather good. Of course, there's no way you'd beat someone like me."

"Why don't we see?" Lancelot replied amiably. "There's plenty of time left before the sun goes down."

The prince shook his head. "You must be so tired," he said with an innocent smile. "I wouldn't like to wear you out."

"You wouldn't like to lose, you mean," Elena muttered under her breath, for she knew her brother all too well.

"Then let's make a date in a few weeks' time, when we're both well rested," Lancelot suggested. "I'm game if you are."

A gleam of cunning appeared in the prince's eyes. "What a good idea," he said. "Let's say Midsummer's Day at King Arthur's court. Invite lots of people – make sure that all your biggest fans are there." And he stalked off across the field.

The next day, as Lancelot was setting off for home, a maid rushed up to him. "My mistress has been taken prisoner by a mighty knight," she said. "Only you could possibly save her."

"I'll do my best," Lancelot promised, and he rode off with the maid right away to see what he could do.

Weeks passed by and he did not return home. "It's not like Lancelot to be gone so long," King Arthur said, looking worried.

"He must be caught up in some adventure," Gawain, Lancelot's best friend, reassured him. "He'll be back in time to meet Prince Maurice's challenge."

Word about the challenge had spread, and on Midsummer's Day eager crowds gathered around the jousting field to see the battle. But there was still no sign of Lancelot.

Prince Maurice rode onto the field wearing armor so shiny it looked as if it had never been used. "Is Lancelot ready for our little fight?" he asked.

"Lancelot's missing," Gawain replied dejectedly. "He never came home from your father's spring tournament."

"That's when I challenged him to fight. He's run away," crowed the prince. "What a coward!"

Gawain flushed with anger at the insult to his friend. "Lancelot's no coward," he retorted.

"Let him prove it," smirked the prince. "I'll give him until next Midsummer's Day to pluck up some courage. If he doesn't show up then, everyone will know for sure that he's afraid of me."

He galloped all the way to his father's castle and burst into the hall, where the king was holding court. "Lancelot's a coward," he announced triumphantly to all the people gathered there. "He's run away."

The king frowned at his son. "You're a boasting fool," he said. "There's no way a brave knight like Lancelot would run away. He must be helping someone in trouble, or else he's in some kind of trouble himself."

At that, the prince turned bright red and stormed out of the hall.

Princess Elena was beside her father and had seen the whole thing. Her brother's reaction made her uneasy. "I bet Maurice has got something to do with Lancelot's disappearance," she thought. "I hope he hasn't done anything awful." She put on her cloak, saddled her horse and set off to look for Lancelot.

Elena searched every last corner of her father's kingdom. She rode over mountains and through valleys, across plains and into forests, asking everyone she met if they'd seen the knight. There wasn't a trace of Lancelot anywhere, but the princess swore she'd never give up until she found him.

One dull morning, she was riding along a remote stretch of coastline when she saw a tall, black tower perched on the edge of a cliff. It was a very peculiar tower – it had no door or entrance of any sort. High up, near the top, the princess could just about see the tiniest slit of a window.

She got off her horse and shouted up to the window, "Is anybody there?" She listened, but there was no reply. She cupped her hands around her mouth and shouted louder. "Lancelot! Are you in there?"

This time, a faint voice floated back in reply. "Yes," it called. "Prince Maurice tricked me into believing a lady was trapped in the tower. When I climbed the steps to rescue her, he walled me in and left me here to starve."

"Take heart," called the princess. "I'm going to save you." She looked at the tower and pondered for a moment. Then she called, "I'll be back soon," and hurried away on her horse.

Within the hour, she was back. With her she brought a bow and arrow, a rope and an ax. She tied the rope to the end of the arrow. "Move away from the window," she called to Lancelot. Then she took careful aim and fired. The arrow sailed through the air and straight through the tiny slit window.

"Tie the rope to something," Elena called. She waited for Lancelot to do as she asked, and then tugged on the rope to make sure it was secure. Then she tied the end around her waist, tucked the ax into her belt and began to scale the wall.

It was a terrifying climb. The wind howled around the tower, threatening to blow her off; her arms and legs ached and her fingers bled from clinging to the stones.

Eventually, the princess reached the tiny window. She put her face to the slit and peered in. Tears sprang to her eyes when she saw Lancelot smiling back at her; he was so thin he was almost a skeleton.

She set to work, chipping away at the stone with her ax. It was hard going, but after two hours she had made the slit big enough for Lancelot to squeeze through. Together, they lowered themselves slowly to the ground.

The princess took Lancelot to one of her father's castles to recover. She told no one he was there, but took care of him in secret. Slowly but surely, Lancelot regained his strength.

Meanwhile, life at King Arthur's court went on as usual, but the joy had gone from everyone's hearts. People waited anxiously for news of Lancelot, fearing that some day they would hear of his death.

Midsummer's Day came around again and a despondent crowd gathered on the jousting field to see what would happen. Prince Maurice arrived, wearing a confident sneer on his face. "Is the coward still in hiding?" he asked as he galloped onto the field.

Gawain was waiting for him. "Enough of your insults," he said firmly. "Lancelot isn't here, but I'll fight you on his behalf."

At that very moment, a knight galloped onto the field with a girl at his side. "Thanks Gawain, but I think I should fight my own battles," he said, and took off his helmet. "Lancelot," Gawain shouted joyfully, "you're alive!" And the crowd cheered.

The prince's smug smile froze on his face. "H-how did you escape?" he stammered in shock. But then his brow knitted as he saw his sister. "You traitor," he hissed at her.

"You're a traitor to yourself," Elena retorted hotly, "and to our entire kingdom. I'm ashamed to call you my brother. You're going to fight Lancelot right this minute, and we can put an end to this nonsense."

Maurice turned pale. "All right," he said in a small voice.

The two men got into position and the crowd fell silent. Gawain sounded the trumpet, and Lancelot and the prince galloped towards one another.

Prince Maurice had never been much good at jousting. His lance wobbled as he took aim, and he completely forgot to hold up his shield. With one thrust of his lance, Lancelot toppled him from his saddle.

"There," said Lancelot, "that settles it."

"No it doesn't!" screeched Maurice, his face burning red with shame and rage. "You might be better than me with a lance, but I could kill you with a single swipe of my sword."

Lancelot gave him a cool stare. "Let's see," he said. He got down from his horse and drew his sword. "Ready?" he asked. The prince nodded, and Lancelot swung at him.

But Maurice was an appalling sword-fighter too. He slashed back clumsily and tripped over his own feet. Lancelot waited until he had regained his balance, and allowed him to take the next swing.

Maurice swiped at Lancelot's head with his blade. Lancelot deflected it easily and landed a heavy blow on the prince's chest. Then, in one deft move, he knocked the prince's sword and shield flying, leaving him completely and utterly defenseless.

Without waiting to see what would happen next, Prince Maurice turned tail and fled. He hopped onto his horse and galloped for all he was worth out of the field, away from the kingdom and all the way home.

The onlookers burst into gales of laughter as they watched the prince disappear into the distance. Maurice never dared show his face in King Arthur's kingdom again, but his sister, Princess Elena, was loved throughout the land.

Gawain's ugly bride

King Arthur was out riding on Christmas morning when he came upon an eerie black castle, which he'd never seen before. There was a man in a long, dark cloak standing on the drawbridge. "Good morning," Arthur called, but the man just turned away and started walking back towards the castle.

King Arthur rode after him. As soon as his horse stepped onto the drawbridge, he felt a strange buzzing sensation in his ears, and all the energy drained from his body. "What kind of sorcery is this?" he gasped, slumping helplessly over his horse's neck.

"So this is the powerful King Arthur," a bone-chilling voice whispered in his ear. "Well, you're in *my* power now."

The sorcerer peered into Arthur's face. "I'm going to take your kingdom and your life," he hissed. "Who would have thought it could be so simple?"

"You coward," the king retorted defiantly, although he could barely move.

The sorcerer's mouth twisted into a smile. "Actually," he replied, "it's no challenge beating you so very easily."

His eyes glinted with cunning. "I'll let you go," he said, "if you promise to return on New Year's Day with the answer to my riddle. If you fail to answer correctly, you'll lose your kingdom and your life."

"You have my word," said Arthur.

"Good," said the sorcerer. "Then here's the riddle: all the world over, under every roof and spire, what is the one thing that women most desire?" He laughed scornfully. "You'll never find the answer," he said. "I look forward to seeing you on New Year's Day." He snapped his fingers, and he and his entire castle vanished into thin air.

In the days that followed, the king searched his kingdom for the answer to the riddle. He asked the cleverest ladies and the lowliest serving maids in his castle, and he sent his knights the length and breadth of the land to ask all the women they met what it was they most desired.

But every woman's answer was different from the last. Some said "fine dresses" and others said "beauty"; some said "wisdom" and others said "gold"; some said "a brave knight to love" and others said "a castle to call their very own".

New Year's Eve arrived and Arthur was still no closer to finding the answer. "Time is running out," the king said in despair. "None of these can be the one thing that *all* women desire."

"Don't worry," said Gawain, the king's most loyal knight. "I'll find the answer for you somehow." And he set off on his horse to scour the kingdom once again. All day long he rode, asking every single girl, mother and grandmother he came across, "What is it that women most desire?"

Slowly, the sun turned blood-red and sank behind the trees. Gawain stopped to rest, his head spinning with all the answers he'd heard – clever children, good health, less washing, more free time... "I still don't have the one true answer," he said, shaking his head. "But there's no one left to ask."

"You haven't asked me," said a croaky voice.

Gawain looked up and almost fell off his horse in shock. Sitting on a tree stump by the side of the road was the most hideous woman he'd ever seen. She had a long, warty nose with hairs sprouting from it; her eyes were sunken and bloodshot, and her mouth was filled with crooked black teeth.

Gawain got down from his horse. "Good lady," he said politely. "If you could tell me what it is that women most desire, I would be eternally grateful."

"I can give you the answer," replied the woman, "and save the king and the kingdom from the grasp of that evil sorcerer. But if I help you, you must promise me you'll do one thing."

"What's that?" asked Gawain.

The ugly creature heaved herself to her feet and hobbled closer. Gawain tried not to flinch as his nostrils filled with the vilest stench imaginable. She leered at him, and a drop of spit dribbled down her chin. "Marry me," she said.

Gawain froze in horror. Then he thought of the king, whom he loved dearly, and the kingdom he was supposed to help protect. "All right," he said quietly. "I'll marry you."

"Splendid," cackled the woman, and she whispered the answer into his ear.

"Thank you," said Gawain. He helped the hag onto his horse, put his arms around her waist and galloped home.

The next day, King Arthur went back to see the sorcerer. He found the black castle in the same spot as before. "Come out," he commanded.

The sorcerer appeared on the drawbridge. "Ready to hand over your kingdom?" he asked smugly.

"No," answered Arthur. "I have the answer to your riddle."

The sorcerer's face fell.

"The thing that women most desire," Arthur continued, "is the freedom to choose for themselves."

The sorcerer clenched his fists and trembled with rage. "Who told you?" he shrieked.

But the king didn't reply. He simply turned his back and set off for home – he had a wedding to attend.

Back at the castle, everybody had already gathered in the chapel for the marriage ceremony. As Arthur joined Queen Guinevere at the front, he noticed that there were more ladies weeping than was usual at a wedding. Even Guinevere had tears in her eyes. "Poor Gawain," she sighed, "having to marry that hideous crone. I'm surprised he isn't in tears himself."

But Gawain didn't weep. He waited patiently at the front of the chapel as his bride shuffled down the aisle, staring rudely at everyone she passed. She hadn't even bothered to bathe for the occasion. The smell was so great that a swarm of flies buzzed around her, and one or two ladies fainted clean away as she passed by.

Despite her horrible appearance, Gawain took his bride's hand gently and swore to love and protect her until the end of his life. Before the bell had pealed for twelve o'clock, they were husband and wife.

The wedding feast was a strange and sorry celebration. None of the guests could bring themselves to eat much, but the bride ate enough for all of them put together. In the first five minutes, she had devoured three chickens and half a leg of beef, swallowed a whole roast pheasant and guzzled a jugful of gravy.

"More," she demanded, wiping her greasy chin with the sleeve of her dress. Even the king felt slightly queasy watching her.

However, Gawain didn't treat his new wife as anything less than a lady. He served her himself, filling her plate with everything she desired, until she slumped back in her chair and burped with satisfaction.

"I think I'll go and get ready for bed," she said at last, and she pushed back her chair and waddled gracelessly out of the hall.

All eyes turned to Gawain in sympathy. A few minutes later, he excused himself from the table and followed his wife upstairs. Outside the room, he paused and took a deep breath; then he knocked on the door.

"Come in," said a soft voice.

When Gawain opened the door, he found a young maiden sitting on the bed in a white nightgown. He blushed, for she was extraordinarily beautiful. "Who are you?" he blurted out.

"Your bride, of course," replied the maiden.

"I— I think I have the wrong room," Gawain stammered in disbelief. The girl before him had smooth golden skin and wide brown eyes. Her lips were cherry red and her chestnut hair shone as it tumbled around her shoulders. She couldn't have been less like the creature he'd just married.

"This is the right room," said the maiden. "I appeared horrible before because of a spell cast upon me by an evil sorcerer. He asked me to marry him and, when I refused, he turned me into a horrible hag, so that nobody else would ever want me." She looked up and gave Gawain a warm smile. "But with your kindness," she continued, "you've defeated the spell...at least in part."

"What do you mean?" asked Gawain.

"I can appear as my true self either at night or in the daytime, but the rest of the time I will be hideous," the maiden replied sadly. "The choice is yours."

54

Gawain walked over to the window and stared out into the starry sky. He thought long and hard. Would it be better to bear the pitying looks of people during the day, if his bride turned into this vision of loveliness when they were alone at night? Or would it be better for everyone to know how lovely she really was, and hide her hideous side away?

He turned to the maiden, who was waiting calmly for him to decide her fate, and his heart nearly burst with pity. It was she who had to live like this. Suddenly, he knew what his answer would be. Kneeling down by the bed, he took her hands in his. "You should choose for yourself," he said. "Whichever you decide, I shall love you just the same."

The maiden's face lit up. "You couldn't have given a better answer," she cried, wrapping her arms around Gawain's neck. "By giving me the freedom to decide for myself, you've broken the spell completely. Now I can stay my true self all the time."

Gawain, of course, was overjoyed. And from that moment on there never was a happier couple.

The kitchen-boy knight

"There's someone here to see you," announced a squire, just as King Arthur and his knights were sitting down for dinner.

A young man was shown in, and he bowed politely to the king. "I'm sorry if I'm disturbing you," he said.

"Not at all," said Arthur. "What brings you here?"

"I have three requests," said the young man. "I hope I'm not asking too much. The first is that I may live in your castle for a year, working in the kitchen to earn my keep."

"I don't see any reason why not," Arthur answered kindly. "What are your other two requests?"

"I know it's a little strange," said the young man, "but if you don't mind, I'd like to tell you after the year has passed."

Arthur laughed good-naturedly. "I don't mind," he said, "although I must confess I'm intrigued. What's your name?"

"I'd rather not say just yet," the young man replied.

"Pah!" snorted Sir Kay, who was sitting next to Arthur. "Who do you think you are, you young upstart? For all we know, you could be an enemy spy."

King Arthur looked hard into the young man's eyes. Then he leaned back in his chair and said, "I think I can trust him, Kay." He nodded at the young man. "You may stay," he said. "We'll speak again in a year's time."

For the next year, the young man lived in the castle as

a kitchen boy. He worked hard at every task he was given, no matter how dirty or dull it was. But Kay lost no opportunity to mock him. "Mind you don't get any ideas above your station, boy," he scoffed as he walked past the kitchen.

Most of the other knights had nothing to do with the kitchen boy, but Lancelot and his friend Gawain often stopped to talk to him. Sometimes, they even tried to persuade him to have dinner with them. The boy was friendly in return, although he never accepted their offer. He always ate in the kitchen with the other servants.

When exactly a year had passed, King Arthur called the kitchen boy into the hall, where all his knights were gathered. "Tell us," said the king, "what are your two other requests?"

Suddenly, a lady burst into the room. "Please help me," she begged. "My sister has been taken prisoner by the Red Knight."

"I know that tyrant," Gawain said darkly. "I fought him once and barely escaped with my life."

"You were lucky to escape at all," said Lancelot. "They say he has the strength of seven men."

The kitchen boy stepped forward. "I'm sorry to interrupt," he said, "but my next request might be of use."

"Go on," said King Arthur.

"May I go on this quest to rescue the lady's sister?" asked the kitchen boy.

"Certainly," said King Arthur.

"Certainly not!" retorted the lady. "A kitchen boy to save my sister? It's out of the question."

"I think he may surprise you," said King Arthur. "Only an exceptionally brave man would offer to fight the Red Knight." He turned back to the kitchen boy. "I'm curious," he said. "Why did you want to spend a year working in my kitchen?"

"To see which of your knights I could count on as true friends," replied the young man, "which leads me to my third request. I'd like Sir Lancelot to follow me on my quest, and to make me a knight if I prove worthy."

"Make a kitchen boy a knight?" Kay spluttered.

"'I'd be delighted," said Lancelot.

"My sister will never be saved at this rate," snorted the lady, and she flounced out of the hall in disgust.

Lancelot went and got the kitchen boy a sword and a horse, and together they hurried after the lady.

"I don't know why you're following me," she said when the kitchen boy caught up with her. "You've no business trying to save my sister."

"I *will* save her, just you wait and see," said the kitchen boy.

They rode on in silence until they came to a river. A knight dressed all in black barred their way. "Don't come any closer," he warned the kitchen boy, "or I'll have to fight you."

"Please do," said the lady. "Chase this scoundrel back to the kitchen he came from."

Without further ado, the Black Knight charged. The kitchen boy watched him thunder closer. Then, at the very last moment, he darted to one side, seized the knight's lance and wrenched him from his horse. Before the Black Knight could get back on his feet, the kitchen boy had a sword at his throat.

"Spare me!" the Black Knight cried.

"I will," said the kitchen boy, "but I'll have to take your armor, your lance and your shield, for I haven't any of my own."

Lancelot, who had been watching from a distance, began to clap. "Bravo," he said. "I'd be proud to knight you after that."

So the kitchen boy put on the Black Knight's armor and knelt before Lancelot. "Arise, Sir..." Lancelot began, but then he stopped and smiled. "I don't know your name," he said.

The kitchen boy glanced at the lady, who was busy staring down her nose at him, and then whispered his name into Lancelot's ear. "Please don't tell anyone else just yet," he said. "I'd like to prove myself properly first."

"I won't tell a soul," promised Lancelot. "Arise, Sir—" and he whispered the rest, so the others couldn't hear. "Good luck with your quest," he said. "I'll ride back and tell King Arthur that you've proved yourself a worthy knight."

"Beginner's luck," scoffed the lady. She spurred her horse onward, and the kitchen-boy knight followed her.

A little way along the path, they came across a knight dressed all in green. "My dear brother," the knight called out when he saw the kitchen-boy knight's black armor.

"This isn't your brother," said the lady. "This so-called knight beat the Black Knight and stole his armor. And I, for one, think you should beat him to a pulp for it."

The Green Knight frowned. "I will," he said, and he charged. The kitchen-boy knight trotted forward and, with one deft thrust of his lance, knocked his opponent right off his horse. The Green Knight somersaulted through the air and landed on his head. He was too dazed to speak for the first five minutes. When he finally did, he simply croaked, "You win."

"What is the world coming to when a cockroach like this can beat a real knight?" said the lady indignantly. Tossing her head, she trotted away in a huff.

The kitchen-boy knight rode after her without a word.

Late in the afternoon, they came to a meadow. On a tree at the edge of the meadow hung a shield and a lance, both the color of indigo.

"Now you've met your match," said the lady. "The Indigo Knight is stronger than those other two put together, and he challenges every knight who passes through this field to joust. Hurry back to your kitchen if you want to save your skin."

"I want to save your sister," said the kitchen-boy knight firmly. "I'll fight the Indigo Knight, the Red Knight and any other knight in order to do so." He trotted onto the meadow.

At once, a barrel-chested knight came galloping towards them. But he stopped in his tracks when he saw the kitchen-boy knight. "You're barely more than a child," he said.

"Don't worry about that," replied the kitchen-boy knight, flipping down the visor of his helmet. "I'm stronger than I look."

"If you say so," said the Indigo Knight, and he picked up his shield and lance.

The two knights trotted away from one another and then wheeled around and charged. Their lances slammed into each other's shields and, with a deafening crack, both lances snapped clean in half.

Flinging the broken pieces aside, the knights jumped off their horses and drew their swords. Back and forth they fought, their blades flashing in the crimson light of the setting sun, until they were panting with exhaustion.

Finally, the kitchen-boy knight dealt the Indigo Knight a spirited blow that sent him tumbling to the ground.

"You win," groaned the Indigo Knight. "I've never met such a worthy opponent – I'd hate to have you as my enemy."

"There's no reason we can't be friends," replied the kitchen-boy knight. He sheathed his sword and helped the Indigo Knight to his feet.

The lady, who had been watching the battle thoughtfully, got down from her horse. She stood before the kitchen-boy knight and hung her head in shame. "I've treated you horribly," she said. "I'm very, very sorry. The truth is you're the bravest knight I've ever met. Can you forgive me?"

"Of course I can," said the kitchen-boy knight, looking relieved. "Let's forget all about it."

Together, they rode to the Indigo Knight's castle, where he gave them a fine supper and comfortable beds for the night. In the morning, with the gift of a new lance from their host, they continued their journey to rescue the lady's sister.

They found the Red Knight's castle looming above the sea, with blood-red flags flying from every tower. As they rode towards it, the kitchen-boy knight saw something that made even him turn pale. From the branches of a tall tree hung dozens of dead knights.

"That's what he does to any knight who dares challenge him," murmured the lady. "It's not too late for you to turn back."

"And leave your sister with that tyrant?" said the kitchen-boy knight. "Never." He rode up to the castle and shouted, "Red Knight, I demand you set this lady's sister free."

The Red Knight, a terrifying hulk of a man, appeared on the drawbridge. "I will not," he roared. "But I'll gladly hang you on my tree." He spurred his horse and galloped headlong at the kitchen-boy knight.

The kitchen-boy knight sped fearlessly towards him, and the two collided with such force that both of their horses fell from under them.

Barely pausing to catch their breath, they drew their swords and threw themselves at one another. The Red Knight really did have the strength of seven men. He dealt such mighty blows that sparks flew from the kitchen-boy knight's armor. Before long, the kitchen-boy knight's shield was cracked and splintered, and his battered armor hung in useless pieces from his shoulders.

He fought on doggedly until he was so tired he could barely swing his sword. With one merciless blow after another, the Red Knight beat him to the ground.

All seemed lost. Then, just as the Red Knight raised his sword to finish the kitchen-boy knight off, the lady cried, "You're not going to let this monster win, are you?"

It was just what the kitchen-boy knight needed. With a fresh surge of energy, he flipped the Red Knight onto his back, sending his sword skittering away, and then pounced on top of him. At once, the Red Knight's courage crumbled. "Have mercy," he whimpered, "I beg you."

The kitchen-boy knight paused. "If I kill you after you've begged for mercy, I'm no better than you are," he said. "I'll spare you on one condition – that you serve this lady and her sister until the end of your days."

The Red Knight nodded. "I promise I will," he said.

"You did it!" the lady cried. "Well done, kitchen boy." Then she stopped and blushed bright red. "I can't keep on calling you that," she said. "What's your real name?"

"Prince Gareth," replied the kitchen-boy knight.

The lady gasped. "Why didn't you *say* so?" she said.

"I didn't want people to think well of me just because I'm a prince," replied the kitchen-boy knight. "I wanted to earn my good name."

"Well, you've certainly done that," said the lady. "Now let's go and free my sister."

King Arthur
and the
magic barge

A pure white stag fled through the forest with three men on horseback in hot pursuit. King Arthur, King Uryens and Sir Accolon had been chasing the stag for several hours. It led them deeper and deeper into the forest, always leaping just out of reach. Following at breakneck speed, desperate to keep it in their sight, the men paid no attention to where they were going. Suddenly, in the dark heart of the forest, the creature disappeared.

Looking around, the men realized that they were lost. Daylight was fading fast and soon it would be dark. "We'll never find our way back home tonight," said King Arthur. "Let's find somewhere to rest until morning."

As he turned to lead the way, he caught sight of something glinting between the trees. He pushed through the branches to find a large, still lake. A beautiful barge was tethered to the shore.

"Is anybody there?" called Arthur. There was no answer, so he stepped cautiously onto the barge. Immediately, a hundred torches blazed to life. Shadows danced in the flickering light but, strangely, there was not a soul to be seen.

67

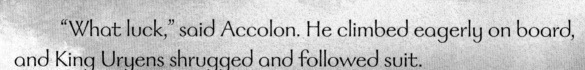

"What luck," said Accolon. He climbed eagerly on board, and King Uryens shrugged and followed suit.

"Look," breathed Arthur. Right before his eyes, twelve enchanting maidens had appeared. They had golden hair and emerald-green eyes – in fact, they were all utterly identical.

"Welcome," they chorused in soft, musical voices. "The forest is a dangerous place after dark. You may stay here until morning, if it pleases you."

"Thank you," said Arthur. One of the maidens waved her hand, and a table appeared with a feast laid out on it. The men were ravenous, and so, without a second thought, they sat down and ate. Slowly, the sky turned inky black above them.

68

After they had eaten their fill, the men felt very, very sleepy. The maidens spread soft, silk cushions out on the deck for them to lie down, and all three men sank into a deep and dreamless sleep.

In the morning, King Uryens was the first to wake up. To his astonishment, he found that he was at home in his own castle, lying in his very own bed. "How did I end up here?" he murmured to himself.

He looked around and saw his wife, the sorceress Morgan le Fay, lying next to him. She had a cunning look on her face that he recognized only too well. "Morgan," he said in alarm, "What have you done...?"

69

Meanwhile, on the other side of the kingdom, King Arthur was waking up, stiff and groggy, on a cold, damp floor. It was very dark, but as far as he could tell he was in some kind of castle dungeon. He was chained to the wall, and could just make out the shapes of other prisoners around him.

At that moment, the bolts slid back on the door and a maid appeared. "I am here to offer you a choice," she said. "You may fight in a battle to the death, for the amusement of my lord and his friend, or rot in this dungeon until someone else comes along who is brave enough to accept the challenge."

"I'd rather die in battle than in this pit of a place," said Arthur boldly. "I will fight — but on two conditions."

"What are they?" asked the maid.

"First," replied Arthur, "that my sword, Excalibur, is brought to me before the battle and, second, that if I win, all these prisoners will be set free."

"I'm sure that can be arranged," said the maid. "Until later, then." She swung the heavy door shut, plunging Arthur and the other men back into pitch darkness.

In a nearby meadow,
Sir Accolon was rubbing his eyes
in disbelief. Before him stood a dwarf,
holding out a sword with intricate engravings all
along its scabbard. "King Arthur's sister, Morgan le Fay, sent
me," the dwarf said.

Accolon took hold of the scabbard and drew the sword.
Its blade shone brilliantly in the sunlight and a surge of energy
rushed through his body, making him stagger backwards.

"It's Excalibur, King Arthur's magic sword," explained the
dwarf. "It will give you immense power in battle. And if you wear
the scabbard it will protect you from all wounds. Morgan le Fay
would like you to use it to fight in a battle this afternoon."

"What battle?" asked Sir Accolon in surprise.

"A wicked lord has taken King Arthur captive," replied
the dwarf. "You must fight him to the death to save the king."

Accolon put the sword back into its scabbard and buckled it around his waist. "Lead the way," he said gravely.

When they arrived at the castle, crowds were already gathering to watch the battle. A suit of armor was waiting at the side of the field. The dwarf helped Accolon put it on; then he brought the knight a horse, a green shield and a lance.

With the magic sword at his side, Accolon rode onto the jousting field feeling invincible. He could see his opponent on the other side of the field, but the man's face was hidden behind the visor of his helmet, and Accolon didn't recognize him. "Who is this evil lord?" Accolon wondered. Then he shrugged his shoulders. "No matter," he thought. "He's captured my king. That's all I need to know."

On the other side of the field, King Arthur eyed up his opponent, not for a moment suspecting it was Accolon. A squire presented him with a sword in an intricately engraved scabbard. "Your loving sister sends your sword, Excalibur, and her best wishes for the battle," he said, nodding in the direction of a hooded lady in the crowd.

Arthur frowned. He wasn't sure how much he trusted his magical, meddling sister. As he strapped the sword around his waist, he noticed that it felt lighter than usual. "Something's not right..." he thought. But just then, the herald blew his trumpet. The tournament had begun.

Shaking off his doubts, Arthur gripped his shield, lowered his lance and galloped at the other knight.

The two knights raced at one another, their horses' hooves throwing up clods of mud. Arthur took aim and, with a powerful thrust, toppled Accolon from his horse.

Accolon sprang to his feet unharmed and drew his sword. Arthur leaped down too and launched an immediate attack.

King Arthur was as strong as a lion and as quick as lightning. For every ten blows he struck, Accolon only managed one. The crowd was speechless with awe.

Yet, no matter how hard Arthur struck, no harm seemed to come to his opponent, while each blow Arthur received sliced through his armor as though it were made of paper.

Before long, people in the crowd began to mutter in confusion. How could the better knight be losing?

Redoubling his efforts, Arthur swung a hefty blow at his opponent. Accolon quickly raised his sword to meet it, and Arthur's blade snapped off at the hilt. Arthur stared at it in horror. "How can that be possible?" he thought. "Excalibur can't break."

Nonetheless, he faced his opponent with the broken sword. So great was his skill, that he still managed to parry Accolon's blows. But he couldn't get close enough to attack, and his wounds were sapping his strength.

Then, suddenly, he spotted his opponent's engraved scabbard. He stared in bewilderment. It was exactly the same as his own. When he looked at the sword in the other knight's hand, the truth suddenly hit him. "That's my sword," he roared.

With a surge of fury, Arthur slammed his shield into Accolon's chest and knocked the magic sword flying from his hand.

Everybody watched with baited breath as Excalibur spun high into the air. Then King Arthur reached up and caught the sword. The crowd erupted with excitement.

A familiar surge of energy ran through Arthur's body as his fingers closed around the hilt of his sword. "That's more like it," he thought.

Before Accolon even had time to move, Arthur tore the magic scabbard from his waist. "I've suffered too much from my own sword," he muttered. "Now it's your turn." And he struck down his opponent with a single blow.

"You fight as if justice is on your side," groaned Accolon, "even though you have captured my king."

Arthur started at the sound of the man's voice. "Tell me your name," he demanded, "and where you got this sword."

"My name is Accolon," came the reply. "Morgan le Fay lent me the sword to save King Arthur from imprisonment."

"Morgan did this?" gasped Arthur.

A strangled cry came from the crowd. Arthur looked up and saw Morgan le Fay fling back the hood of her cloak. She glared at him with hatred burning in her eyes.

"My own sister," said Arthur, his voice simmering with anger. "I never thought you'd go this far."

"My lord?" Accolon whispered fearfully. "Is that really you?"

Arthur pulled off his helmet. A murmur rippled around the crowd as everyone realized who he was.

"I s-s-swear," stammered Accolon, "I didn't know it was you. I never would have agreed to fight my own king."

"I believe you," said Arthur. "We've both been tricked by my murderous sister." He fixed Morgan with a steely gaze. "Would you care to explain why you're set on trying to kill me?" he asked her.

"I don't need to explain anything to you," the sorceress replied bitterly. "What makes you so special? I have magic at my fingertips – the power to conjure up gold-haired beauties and whisk people from place to place while they sleep. But it's you who have everything. No matter what happens, you always manage to come out on top."

"This isn't a game, sister," said Arthur sternly. "This is real life. You can't play with people's lives."

"Bah! What's real?" retorted Morgan. "Was the food you ate on the barge real? Or the barge itself? Or this?" She drew a shape in the air with her fingers and storm clouds gathered, forming the shape of a dragon in the sky.

Suddenly, the dragon dived. The crowd stumbled around in panic, bumping into one another and screaming in terror.

But before the dragon reached the ground, it dissolved into harmless wisps of cloud. By that time, the sorceress had slipped away in the commotion. Arthur, wise to his sister's tricks, was the only one to see her go.

Orfeo
and
his harp

It was a bright spring morning and Queen Isabel was sitting beneath a shady tree in the castle garden. Orfeo, her husband, was playing his harp inside the castle, and the music floated down on the breeze to where she was sitting. He played so beautifully that even the birds had stopped singing to listen. Isabel closed her eyes and let out a happy sigh. Before she knew it, she had drifted off to sleep.

A little later, Orfeo heard his wife scream. He rushed into the garden and found her sitting under the tree. She was as pale as a ghost and trembling with fright. "What's wrong?" he asked, putting his arms around her.

The queen wept as though her heart would break. Orfeo was desperately worried, but he waited patiently until she was calm enough to speak.

"Something terrible has happened," Isabel said at last. "I have to go away."

"Then I'll come with you," Orfeo replied.

The queen burst into tears again. "You can't," she sobbed. "I have to go alone." Then she explained what had happened.

While she was lying in the shade, a strange and beautiful fairy king had come riding by, accompanied by a hundred fairy knights and maidens, all dressed in shimmering clothes. The king stopped by the tree and smiled at her. "Come with me," he said in a silken voice, "and you shall live in a world more wonderful than anything you have ever imagined."

Bewitched by the fairies' beauty, the queen stood up and walked a little closer to them. The fairy king reached out his hand, but she backed away and shook her head. "I'm happy here," she said. "I have everything I could possibly need. I don't want to come with you."

The fairy king's eyes glittered dangerously. He waved his hand and suddenly Isabel found herself sitting on his horse in front of him. He flicked his reins and they galloped away. The world sped by in a blur, and in no time at all they arrived at the fairy king's castle. Isabel had never seen anything like it. Its walls were as smooth as glass and it had hundreds of crystal towers that sparkled so brightly she could barely look at them.

"This is my kingdom," the fairy king whispered in her ear. "Come inside and live with me forevermore."

"No!" cried the queen.

"You have until tomorrow to change your mind," replied the fairy king. "I'll meet you under the same tree at noon. If you don't come, I'll find you and tear you into tiny pieces. Living or dead, tomorrow you will be mine." Then he whirled his horse around and took her home.

When the queen had finished telling her strange story, King Orfeo took charge. The next morning, he and his wife, and a thousand knights marched into the castle garden to await the fairy king. Isabel stood beneath the tree, holding her husband's hand. The knights surrounded them, gleaming swords at the ready, all determined to protect their beloved queen. "Don't worry, Isabel," said Orfeo. "Who could possibly steal you away now?"

At the stroke of twelve, the king felt the queen's hand slip from his own. He spun around, but she had vanished in the blink of an eye.

"Search the gardens!" Orfeo ordered, and all the knights ran around in confusion.

They hunted high and low all through that day and the next. But the queen had been snatched away by fairy magic, and there was not a single thing anyone could do.

Orfeo locked himself away in his room. After a week had passed, he emerged. His cheeks were hollow and his eyes had lost their sparkle. "I cannot go on living here without my queen," he announced. "I'm going to live in the forest among the trees and the wild beasts."

His lords, advisers and most loyal knights tried their best to persuade him to stay, but the king had made up his mind. Leaving his most trusted friends in charge, he set off for the forest. He carried with him nothing but his most treasured possession — his harp.

For ten whole years, Orfeo lived like a wild animal. He no longer ate dainty food or slept on soft, white sheets. Instead, he survived on nuts and berries, and slept on a bed of moss. He became thin and pale, and his hair and beard grew until they reached his waist. In all this time, he didn't play a single note on his harp. He had hidden it away in the hollow of a tree — its sweet sound was too much for him to bear.

Then one day, he took out the harp and began to play. He had always played wonderfully but now, filled with his longing, the music that floated from the harp was beyond compare. It drifted through the forest, slipping into every hole and burrow, and all the birds and beasts crept out to listen.

From then on, Orfeo played his harp
every single day. Each time he played, the
music grew more beautiful and, each time,
the forest creatures crept a little closer. Soon,
even the most timid birds would settle on his
shoulders, and shy, dappled deer would lie at
his feet to listen to the music.

One day, as Orfeo was playing, he saw a flash
of white through the trees. Then a group of strange
and beautiful fairy maidens appeared, all dressed in
shimmering clothes and riding snow-white horses.
In their midst was his beloved Isabel.

Her eyes met his for a brief moment and shone
with recognition. But, before he could say a single
word, the fairy maidens turned and galloped
away, taking Isabel with them.

Clutching his harp, Orfeo scrambled to his feet and dashed after them. He ran as fast as his legs would carry him, but it was no use. Horses are fleet of foot, and fairy horses even more so; they got further and further ahead, until they disappeared from view. Orfeo kept on running through the forest, hoping to catch sight of them again, but they had vanished without a trace.

"I can't bear it," he cried, falling to his knees in despair. "How will I ever find her now?" He buried his face in his hands and began to sob.

Just then, something nudged his arm. He looked up and, to his surprise, saw a herd of dappled deer standing before him. He recognized them at once, for it was the same herd that came every day to listen to his music. The largest stag stepped forward. It lowered its head, and then knelt down. It seemed to be inviting Orfeo to climb onto its back.

Orfeo took hold of the creature's antlers and swung his leg over its haunches. The stag rose to its feet and began to run. It ran so lightly that its hooves barely touched the ground. Orfeo felt as though they were flying. He clung tightly to the stag's antlers until finally it slowed to a halt.

The stag had stopped at the edge of the forest. Orfeo gasped, for there before his eyes was a castle just like the one Isabel had described. Its delicate crystal towers sparkled so brightly they dazzled him.

"The fairy kingdom," Orfeo whispered. He slid down from the stag's back. "Thank you, dear friend," he said, stroking the animal's velvety neck.

The noble stag bowed its head, and then slipped back into the forest.

Orfeo made his way to the gates of the castle and knocked loudly. "Who goes there?" called the gatekeeper.

"A musician to play for the king," Orfeo replied.

The gatekeeper opened the gates and let him inside. A dismal sight met Orfeo's eyes. All around the courtyard there were people frozen in various poses – ladies mid-dance, knights on galloping horses, babies in their cradles – each one captured by fairy magic. He looked around quickly, to see if his wife was among them, and his heart leaped as he spotted her lying beneath a tree. She was asleep, just as she had been when the fairy king had seen her for the very first time.

"Come with me," said the gatekeeper. He led Orfeo into a hall where the fairy king was sitting. Orfeo knelt before the king. "My lord," he said, "I've come to play you some music."

"What sort of fool are you to come here?" snapped the fairy king, frowning fiercely. "No one dares come here without an invitation."

"I'm just a wandering minstrel," was Orfeo's humble reply. "It is our custom to call at each castle we pass and offer our music."

Without waiting for the fairy king to speak again, Orfeo began to play his harp. A golden melody rose from his fingers like a charm. The king's frown melted away, and he settled back in his throne to listen. Fairy knights and maidens crept into the hall, enchanted by the music.

As the last note died away, the king sighed. "That was truly extraordinary," he said. "Your playing pleased me very much. Name your reward – whatever you like shall be yours."

"Kind Sir," said Orfeo, "I would like the lady who is sleeping outside beneath a tree."

"Don't be ridiculous!" exclaimed the king. "What would she want with an ugly rogue like you?"

"I think it would be a far uglier thing," replied Orfeo calmly, "for all these fair folk to hear a lie from the lips of their noble king. You said that I could choose any reward."

The king looked uneasy. He glanced around the room at all his fairy subjects. "Take her then," he said bitterly, "and be gone."

Orfeo bowed to the king, and then hurried into the courtyard and knelt beside his wife. Gently, he touched her cheek. Her eyes fluttered open and she smiled, speechless with joy to see him there.

"Come quickly," Orfeo whispered, "before the king changes his mind." They hurried out of the castle and into the forest, where they found the noble stag waiting to take them home.

Isabel and Orfeo lived happily for the rest of their days. And they never, ever saw the fairies again.

The Land of No Return

King Arthur was holding court one morning when a man on horseback burst in through the doors. His horse was black, his armor was black, and his eyes were as black and empty as bottomless pits. "I am the Prince of the Land of No Return," he announced in an icy voice.

Everyone in the room shuddered and the king's face clouded with anger. They all knew people who had ventured into that terrible land and been taken captive. Knight after knight had tried to rescue them, but the prince had sent even the bravest back dead.

"How dare you enter my castle after what you've done?" Arthur thundered. He drew his sword, and there was a hiss of metal as all the knights in the hall drew theirs too. But the prince just sneered. "If you harm me," he said, "your people will be trapped in my land forever. Don't you want to know how to free them?"

"How?" Arthur growled suspiciously.

"If there's a knight who's brave enough," answered the prince, "ask him to escort Queen Guinevere into the forest and do battle with me. If he wins, I'll let the queen return, and set all of the prisoners free. But if he loses, I'll take both him and your charming queen prisoner, and you'll never see them again."

"I'm not risking more innocent lives in your evil games," said Arthur. "Get out of my sight at once!"

The prince shrugged. "I'll be waiting in the forest in case you change your mind," he said, and galloped out of the hall.

Everyone sat for a moment in stunned silence. Then Sir Kay stood up. "If you're going to let him get away with that, I'm leaving," he said.

Queen Guinevere laid her hand on Kay's arm. "We don't want to lose a good knight, especially in these hard times," she said. "What can I do to persuade you to stay?"

"Come with me into the forest," Kay replied, "so that I can beat that prince and set our people free."

Lancelot shot to his feet. "I don't think any of us would want to put the queen at risk, Kay," he said in a warning tone.

Kay ignored him and smiled encouragingly at the queen. "I promise you'll be safe," he coaxed. "I'm the best knight around. There's no way a villain like that could ever beat me."

He looked so sure of himself that Guinevere agreed.

"It's too risky, my love," said King Arthur. "Please don't go."

But the queen wouldn't be dissuaded. "We have to try," she said, and Arthur reluctantly agreed. Holding her head up bravely, Guinevere rode with Kay into the dark forest.

Only a few minutes later, Kay's horse came charging back without a rider. "I knew it," said Arthur, turning deathly pale.

"The prince will have taken them to his castle," said Lancelot. "I'll try to save them." And he galloped off into the forest.

The path to the Land of No Return was completely overgrown, and before long Lancelot's horse could go no further. Lancelot jumped down and drew his sword. He was about to start slashing through the branches when, to his astonishment, they parted on their own.

He stepped forward cautiously, and more branches parted, allowing him to go a little further. As soon as he'd passed through them, the branches wove themselves together again behind him.

Lancelot shuddered; then he hurried on through the trees. After some time, he reached the edge of the forest. As he stepped out into the open, the last few branches knotted themselves together, making it impossible to turn back.

He had come to a small town. Guards swarmed the streets, and everyone he saw looked miserable. A man walked by, leading a horse. "Please could you tell me where I am?" Lancelot asked him.

"The Land of No Return," came the gloomy reply. "I pity you for coming here. Now, like us, you'll never be able to leave."

"I will leave," said Lancelot firmly, "and so will you, once I've defeated the prince."

"You're either a fool or the bravest man alive!" exclaimed the man. "To reach his castle without the aid of magic, you'd have to cross the Sword Bridge. No one has ever survived it."

"I have no choice," said Lancelot urgently. "I have to rescue the queen. Where is this bridge?"

The man pointed beyond the town. "Go that way and let your ears be your guide," he said, looking at Lancelot with respect. "If you really are determined to get there, you'll need a horse. Take mine," he said, handing Lancelot the reins, "and good luck."

"Thank you," said Lancelot. He swung himself into the saddle and galloped out of the sad little town. As he rode, he heard a distant rumble. He sped towards the noise, which grew louder and louder all the time.

At last, he arrived at a deep, rocky gorge. Peering down into the chasm, Lancelot saw where the sound was coming from — far below, an icy black river crashed and tumbled over the jagged rocks. Echoing up from the depths, the noise became a deafening roar.

Across the gorge lay a gigantic sword. It was the strangest bridge Lancelot had ever come across. To test how sharp it was, he picked up a pebble and tossed it onto the gleaming blade. The pebble was sliced in two as easily as if it were made of butter. Lancelot's blood ran cold as the pieces plummeted into the torrent below.

But that wasn't all. On the other side of the Sword Bridge were two ferocious lions. "Even if I do get across," murmured Lancelot, "I'll be eaten alive." Then he thought of the poor queen being held prisoner. Closing his eyes, he took a deep breath and stepped out onto the Sword Bridge.

Lancelot winced as he felt the blade cut through his boots and into the soles of his feet. Gritting his teeth against the pain, he opened his eyes and began to make his way slowly across the gorge.

He had almost made it to the other side when the lions let out a monstrous roar. The sound broke Lancelot's concentration and he lost his balance. For one hair-raising moment, he teetered over the plunging drop. But he kept his nerve and managed to regain his footing.

When he looked up, the lions were eyeing him hungrily. "I can't give up now," thought Lancelot, "even if I die trying." So he drew his sword and leaped off the bridge.

As soon as his feet left the blade, the lions vanished into thin air, and Lancelot tumbled to the ground unharmed. "What enchantment is this?" he gasped in astonishment.

"Nobody has ever managed to cross the Sword Bridge before," snarled a voice high above his head. Lancelot looked up and saw the prince's face at the window of a tower. "Now that you have," the prince said, "you'll have to fight me."

Lancelot got to his feet. "Very well," he said calmly, "but if I defeat you, you must release the queen and all the other prisoners in this land."

The prince glanced at Lancelot's bleeding feet and torn clothing, and a confident smile spread across his face. "All right," he snickered. Then he pulled Guinevere to the window. "And you, my dear queen," he hissed, "can watch."

The prince came down from
the tower and soon the men were
armed and ready to fight.

Lancelot was exhausted,
but one look at the queen's lovely,
anxious face at the top of the tower
was all he needed to give him strength.
With a might rarely seen before or since,
he charged and slammed his lance into
the prince's shield. The lance broke,
splitting the shield in two and
knocking the villain right
out of his saddle.

Glowering, the prince got to his feet and drew his sword. Lancelot jumped to the ground and drew his own. Their blades met with a clash of steel.

"After I've slung you in the dungeon with that other useless knight," the prince panted, "the queen will be mine forever." He leered up at Guinevere, and Lancelot seized his moment. With one deft thrust, he flicked the prince's sword out of his hand, and pinned him against the tower.

"Surrender," Lancelot demanded.

The prince nodded, but his eyes burned with fury. He waited until Lancelot had turned away, then whipped out a dagger and lunged murderously at his back. "I'll kill you first," he snarled.

Lancelot spun around and, in a single swipe, lopped off the prince's head. "No," he said. "You won't."

There was a strange cracking sound, and the locks on the tower and the dungeon sprang open. The prince's evil magic had died along with the villain himself.

"Thank you, Lancelot," the queen said gratefully as she ran down the steps of the tower.

Kay stumbled out of the dungeon, blinking in the sunlight. "The scoundrel took me unawares," he muttered, looking a little disgruntled at having to be rescued. "I'd have beaten him hands down if I'd been ready."

"Never mind about that now, Kay," the queen smiled. "Let's go home."